1859: THE CALM BEFORE THE STORM

A Novella of Colonial Cuba

By Matias Travieso-Diaz

Shawmut Peninsula Press

1859: The Calm Before the Storm

Copyright 2024 © Matias Travieso-Diaz

All rights reserved

Library of Congress Control Number:
2024949625

ISBN: 9798991370448

Shawmut Peninsula Press
Boston, MA

To my daughter

Prologue

La Habana, September 1, 1851

Those who make peaceful revolution impossible will make
violent revolution inevitable.
John F. Kennedy

Alberto Serrano was only six years old when his uncle Leonardo took him to witness the execution of Narciso López. Along with thousands of other spectators, they gathered outside the ancient fortress known as Castillo de La Punta and watched as Spanish guards, escorted López to a specially constructed dais, forced him to sit on a metal chair, shackled him down, and placed an iron collar around his neck. To the boy's horror, the executioner interrupted the prisoner's final words by rotating a bar behind the chair, advancing a screw that tightened the collar, until it strangled López to death. Alberto would forever remember how the prisoner shook violently as he tried to free himself from his bonds while his face turned purple and finally expanded grotesquely. His tongue stuck out as he asphyxiated while the crowd (for the most part) cheered in approval.

Alberto's mother Cecilia had strenuously opposed her brother-in-law's decision to take Alberto to watch the execution, arguing that a child of tender years should not be subjected to such a vicious spectacle, but Alberto's uncle insisted: "It is good that he understands from a very early age that Spain has enemies that must be strongly dealt with. Traitors like López and his crew must be destroyed. Cuba is, and will forever remain, one with the motherland, and any attempts to make us follow the shameful example of the Mexicans and the Colombians will be nipped in the bud."

Cecilia, widowed and depending on the charity of her family, swallowed her concern and yielded to her brother-in-law's demands. Alberto was the youngest and only boy of the three underage children she had been forced to raise alone upon the sudden death from yellow fever of Lázaro, her husband. Taking the child in her arms, she whispered on his ear: "Albertico, you must be strong. You are the only man in our family, so your sisters and I depend on you to do whatever needs to be done to protect us. For now, you must pay attention to your uncle, and always do as he asks. It will be better for all of us."

Alberto could not understand why the execution's victim, a middle-aged White man whose appearance was hardly threatening, deserved such cruel treatment. All the boy was told was that López had led an armed group that came from outside Cuba, landed on a beach west of La Habana, and tried to do something against the government.

Later in life, Alberto would learn that many Cubans wanted independence from Spain, complaining of economic inequality, lingering slavery, and the despotic rule of the governors Spain appointed to rule its last colony in the Americas. Others, particularly the island's White landholders, feared that a revolt would result in a slave uprising (like had happened in Haiti half a century before) or, at a minimum, bring about the abolition of slavery with adverse impacts on their interests. Further complicating matters was the notion, which López and his supporters shared but others did not, that Cuba should become part of the United States instead of an independent nation. Politicians and others in the slave-owning South of the U.S. were in favor of annexing Cuba and supported López, causing his invasion to become entangled with internal American politics.

But as he watched the gruesome execution, Alberto was oblivious of all of that. He only felt, deep in his soul, that whatever had happened that September morning was wrong and upsetting, and he wanted no part of it, and perhaps someday he would do something to prevent it from happening again.

Chapter 1

La Habana, June 1856: Graciela's Debutante Party

I wasn't brought up as a society girl to go to balls and be a debutante and marry the social set and money and go to parties. … I always wanted a career.

Lauren Bacall

The formal party her mother insisted on throwing for her to mark her fifteenth birthday was the greatest imposition Graciela had experienced in her short life. But she understood why her mother and uncle Leonardo wanted to organize such an ostentatious show. For her mother, who grew in poverty and did not have such a celebration, it was a chance to vicariously affirm her life's eventual successes; for Leonardo, who had decided to marry his business instead of a wife, it was the opportunity to display his wealth and achievements before his business contacts and the upper level of the Habana society.

In addition, los quince, the debutante ball, was a critical point in the life of a woman. It signified that the honored girl, the quinceañera, was ready to fulfill her public role in society; to marry, bear children, and provide comfort and support to her husband; and manage their household in a proper and dignified manner. The problem was that Graciela did not feel ready to do any of these things and doubted she would ever want to do them.

She hated housework and was not very good at it. Besides, their household slave María Dolores (who everyone called "Yaya") took care of all the cleaning and could cook and bake better than anyone else. As for finding a man and having and raising children, she was not interested. She might have to do these things someday, but for the moment her attention lay elsewhere.

Graciela wanted to write. Novels. Stories. But mainly poems. She knew by heart many works by classic Cuban bards such as Zequeira and Rubalcava, but her favorites were the new wave of poets led by José María Heredia and Gabriel de la Concepción Valdés, better known as Plácido. Heredia and Plácido attracted her by the formal freedom and the emotional content of their works, and also by the very romantic nature of their lives: both poets had embraced the cause of Cuba's independence, had died young, and had paid with their lives for their ideals. Heredia died in exile, Plácido before a firing squad.

Graciela knew she had to be careful not to be too outspoken in praising these revolutionary poets, for her uncle Leonardo was a strong supporter of the Spanish colonial administration and would have looked askance at any political dissent, expressed or implicit, from within his family. Her sister Carmela, three years younger, was just entering puberty and discovering boys and had no use for politics or the arts. That left only Albertico to serve as a potential confidant. She loved her little brother, but he was too young to be reliable, so her conversations with him had to be guarded for fear he would inadvertently give her oddness away.

Her mother was also no help. Coming from a poor family, she could barely read and write and had no interest in things outside her domestic world. Right now, her main concern was to properly introduce her oldest daughter to the upper-class society in which they moved thanks to Leonardo's wealth and connections. The coming out party, therefore, had to be a success.

***

It took months of arduous preparations to bring about Graciela's party; it was an enterprise in which the entire family collaborated. Except for her.

On a humid Saturday evening in late June, Graciela sat in an open horse-drawn carriage bedecked with garlands of flowers that cruised leisurely along the Malecón, La Habana's seaside promenade. As she waved to the spectators, the livered driver repeatedly honked a horn to draw everyone's attention to the momentous occasion.

When she arrived at the hall where the ball was to be held, Graciela was greeted by Leonardo, who escorted her through an arched entryway and along a red velvet carpet to the large reception room. There, she was met by her mother, pale as a ghost and breathing heavily from anxiety. As protocol required, Graciela bowed to her mother and thanked her for making this beautiful dream come true. Hand in hand, they strolled through the room, greeting the numerous guests who, for the first time, could admire the transformation of a plain girl into a young princess. Graciela, carefully made up and wearing a wide, snow-white dress and elbow-length gloves, had a tiara circling her carefully coiffed hair and a necklace of fake diamonds with matching dangling earrings.

The stroll concluded and Cecilia retreated to the edge of the room; the dance then began. The first dance, with music provided by a band positioned in an adjoining room, was a danza in the style of the eighteenth-century formal dances of the courts in Europe. Leonardo led his niece partly through the piece and then surrendered her to Albertico, who was only eleven but was serving as his older sister's galán. He, and fourteen other invited boys, wore formal black pants and vests, white linen shirts, and cravats.

Following the first dance, fourteen boys and an equal number of girls joined Graciela and Albertico to form a circle to perform a contradanza, another traditional dance in whose steps they had been instructed by a choreographer hired for the occasion and rehearsed for weeks before the event. The boys were dressed in the same manner as Albertico while the girls wore puffy, pastel-colored gowns in the same style as that of the quinceañera.

Together, the fourteen couples constituted a miniature court gathered to render homage to Graciela and Albertico.

Dancing was then opened to the entire congregation and proceeded through a number of dances, mostly African inspired. After a while, at a signal from Leonardo, the music stopped and the dance floor was cleared to allow the wheeling in of a huge multi-tiered cake decorated with candles and featuring figurines of Graciela's court crowned by a small doll representing her, alone at the top tier. There was a collective murmur of admiration accompanied by the entrance of serving slaves who distributed flutes filled with chilled hard cider. Once everyone had a glass at hand, Leonardo toasted: "Let us drink to my beautiful niece Graciela on her special day. May she live up to her name and grace us for many, many years to come." He and the rest of the attendees raised their flutes up in the air and drank. The toast was followed by the serving of canapés, the cutting and distributing of the cake, and more eating, drinking and dancing until the early morning hours.

***

Much later the following morning, the family

met for breakfast to celebrate the event's success. They took turns praising Graciela for her beauty and poise and thanking Leonardo for his generosity in footing the staggering bill. Cecilia commented: "Graciela, it was good of you to suffer through the heat and discomfort of a full night of partying. I am sorry you had to change clothes five times throughout the evening and refresh your makeup on account of the heat."

Graciela waved dismissively and replied, smiling: "Don't worry, mother. It was all worthwhile," while at the same time thinking: *"Those were the only moments I could spend time with my dear Alicia. Thanks heaven for the heat."*

As the last cups of coffee were served, Leonardo rose, and in the same formal tone he had used the night before to toast, announced: "I have great news. Yesterday, I closed on the purchase of an estate not far from Manzanillo. It includes a small ingenio (sugar mill) on the premises, which I intend to modernize and turn into Cuba's most modern mill. I am having the manor house refurbished. It will be ready for occupation before the hurricane season starts in September." He paused to stare at his family. "We are moving to Oriente."

Cecilia was quick to protest: "What are we going to do there? My children have an education to pursue, friends, a life in La Habana."

"I need you all to come with me to help set up our new estate, which I cannot do alone. After a few months, maybe a year, you can come back to La Habana if you wish. You know, I have no other family, and I intend to leave all I own to you and your children. Thus, it is in your interest that this venture succeed, for it will make us quite wealthy. Think of it as an extended vacation in the country." He pounded on the table energetically to underscore his words.

Cecilia was unconvinced but could not oppose her brother-in-law's imperious request. "A few months in the country" might not be that bad, after all.

Chapter 2

Pilón, Oriente, March – May, 1859: Carmela's Quince

There's nothing worse than the sequel that's a letdown from the first movie.
Paul Feig

Much had changed in the three years since Graciela's debutante ball. Their move to the estate in Oriente had caused acrimony within the family. Cecilia and her children had resisted the move and attempted to stay behind, but Leonardo was inflexible: as head of the family after his older brother's untimely passing, he insisted that they all stay together and live in safety and comfort under the same roof, at least for a while.

By the time Cecilia's middle child, Carmela, approached the magic age of fifteen, the family was comfortably settled in the casa de vivienda (manor house) of *Santa Cruz*, a large estate that included the sugar mill. The property was located astride Pilón, a small town in southwestern Oriente province. Pilón lay near a beautiful stretch of coast but was twenty leagues from the nearest city of any size, Manzanillo—too far to reach in a day over a steep mountain road. Santiago de Cuba was 40 leagues away, a several days ride. The distances made opportunities for social interaction with the higher levels of colonial society quite limited.

Cecilia's children were affected by the isolation in various ways. Graciela missed the company of girls her age but shifted her attention to her favorite activities: reading, writing simple poems, and playing the late-model upright piano Leonardo had purchased at great cost to placate his nieces. She hardly noticed the passage of time, at least for the first few years of what she referred to as "our exile in the dark provinces."

Alberto, the most athletic member of the family, went on frequent explorations of the mountains that surrounded Pilón and was soon an expert on the flora of the virgin forests as well as the hollows, caves, and other hiding places that allowed him to escape the his mother's vigilant eye. He was not above making friends with the village youngsters and often engaged in street games of football with other kids his age and older.

It was a motley crowd that gathered for those games. The children of the small village reflected the composition of the local population—a mixture of Spaniards, Black Jamaicans, escaped French colonists from Haiti, White criollos, and descendants of the native Taínos. Alberto, whose amber coloring, slanted eyes, and facial features betrayed his mixed-race heritage, fitted well with the locals and never gave a minute's thought to the race or national origin of his playmates.

Carmela was the one child who was most adversely affected by the move to Pilón. Gregarious by nature, she had left behind a warm circle of friends in La Habana and had great difficulty finding replacements in the small provincial town where she had been forced to live. She found the local teenagers barely educated and quite ignorant of the latest fashions, songs, and dances. For that reason, she limited her infrequent social interactions to a handful of boys and girls, mainly children of mill employees who at least came from good families, even if they were beneath her social standing.

Right after the Easter observances, Cecilia realized she had to do something about Carmela's fast approaching fifteenth birthday. Since everything that cost money depended on Leonardo's approval, the widow reluctantly approached her brother-in-law, who was, as always, busy buying new equipment for the mill and managing the operations of the estate. Their conversation was characteristically brief:

[Cecilia]: "Leonardo, we need to have a party for Carmela. She will turn fifteen in May."

[Leonardo]: "Of course. What did you have in mind?"

[Cecilia]: "It's a problem, because we can't go back to La Habana, and everything we will need for a decent party we can't get around here."

[Leonardo]: "Can you get it in Santiago?"

[Cecilia]: "I suppose, but we would need to seek out vendors and artists, and I don't know anybody there."

[Leonardo]: "Why don't you and Carmela make a shopping trip to Santiago and get what you need? Ruperto can drive you there on our carriage and you can take Yaya along with you. I will write Banco del Comercio to authorize you to withdraw any amounts you need."

[Cecilia]: "Is there any faster way to get to

Santiago than by carriage?"

[Leonardo]: "Sorry, sister. They are starting to build a railway out of Santiago, but it will be years before it cones this way."

[Cecilia (sighing)]: "Is there a limit on the money I can draw?"

[Leonardo]: "Only the balance on my account. But I don't see how you could spend that much."

[Cecilia]: "Thank you. I will be prudent."

[Leonardo]: "Don't worry. Just keep track of how much you draw. Have a nice trip."

***

Cecilia, Carmela, and Yaya were gone for three weeks, including over seven days on the road. It was an exhausting and disappointing trip: Santiago, for all its three and a half centuries of existence, was a provincial town lacking the sophistication of La Habana. It took a lot of effort to make arrangements for what was needed for that special May 29 Sunday, but at the end (after some compromising) they had hired musicians who could play the required dances, caterers to bring and prepare food and a special birthday cake, an expatriate French dressmaker to come to Pilón to fit and create dresses for the girls and suits for the boys who would be accompanying Carmela as her attendants, and a dancing instructor to teach the children new dances, including waltzes.

Now came the hardest part: finding at least half a dozen teenage boys and girls who would be suitable for the occasion. Carmela was privately instructed, but had prevailed on her mother to let her join the local sewing club of which Cecilia was a member and was in reasonably good terms with several girls her age or older, so she was able to find six young women who were willing–indeed, honored–to become participants in the festivities. The boys, however, were a problem: Carmela knew none, and Alberto's football friends were deemed unsuitable by Cecilia, who thought of the lot as mataperros, that is, hooligans. Leonardo had to come to the rescue: he mentioned to his employees and local business associates that he needed to find half a dozen young men of good character to help celebrate his niece's coming of age. He personally interviewed the candidates that were referred to him and selected ten of them, who were then scrutinized by Cecilia, who narrowed the group to half a dozen and invited them to attend the festivities. It was a random array, representing a cross-section of the community's free families, but like other aspects of the celebration of Carmela's quince, it was the best that could be achieved under the circumstances.

As the red-letter day approached, Cecilia was heard to repeat that she and Leonardo were doing their best to duplicate, within the limits of what was possible, the success of the party they had given to Graciela years earlier. Carmela would invariably respond by telling her mother not to worry, she appreciated their efforts but having a grandiose party was not that important to her. And as matters moved along, the excitement grew, not only within the Serrano household but throughout the sleepy village that had never experienced an event of such magnitude.

Alberto was to play the same role for Carmela as he had for their older sister at Graciela's party: he was to be the birthday girl's galán. He would escort Carmela and dance with her a couple of times, but otherwise was not expected to do much entertaining. By now, however, Alberto was fourteen and was beginning to notice girls. So he was looking forward to mingling with members of the fair sex. He discussed his plans with some of his football playmates and extended a broadly worded invitation for them to crash the party:

"I don't think my mom or Uncle Leonardo would do anything to kick you out. Just make sure you wear decent clothes and don't do anything foolish." Most of his friends showed no interest in the party, but a couple of mulatto brothers, Rino and Rodolfito, indicated that they might show up to taste the lechón (roast pork), sample the wedding cake, and drink a glass of wine. "By all means, do come" replied Alberto expansively.

***

As anyone could have predicted, Carmela's party was nowhere near the grandiose event that had been staged for Graciela. There was no carriage ride along Pilón's minuscule waterfront; the lobby of the town's city hall was not designed for large gatherings and could not accommodate more than a couple of dozen occupants; and the town's folks were not sophisticated in the way most residents of La Habana were, so they felt uncomfortable wearing formal dress or doing the modern dance steps. Nonetheless, the invitees were their best behavior and tried to do what was expected of them.

Not all those present behaved as they should. Rino and Rodolfito made good on their promise to crash the party and found themselves standing in the back of the lobby, filching tidbits off the platters as hors d'oeuvres were brought out for the guests. Even they, however, held their breaths expectantly as Carmela was led into the room by her brother.

Carmela was not ugly, but her features were ordinary, and she would not have been cataloged as a beauty. However, for the occasion of her debutante party she had been carefully made up with a thin layer of white powder that lightened her swarthy complexion. Her hair was parted with a ringlet of curls dripping over one shoulder; strands of fragrant jasmine blooms hung from both sides of her head. She was dressed in an off-white full length silk dress with matching laces and flowers and long white silk evening gloves with lace trimmings. Her face was enhanced with darkened lashes and eyebrows, soft rouge on her cheeks, and light pink lip stain. She was wearing gold earrings, a white lace choker from which dangled a dozen seed pearls, and a gold chain holding a starburst gold pendant nesting alternating tiny diamonds and seed pearls. She was a sight that had never been seen in that village, and her entrance elicited an admiring gasp from everyone.

Alberto led his sister in a circuit around the lobby and the two came to stop in the center of the room, at which point a signal was given to the orchestra stationed in a room behind the lobby, and the couple started twirling to the strands of Joseph Lanner's *Die Krönungswalzer*. Brother and sister were experienced dancers, having been trained for two quinceañera parties, but this waltz was a newly learned skill, and they encountered a few stumbling moments, partly due to the unsuitability of the satin evening shoes Carmela was wearing. Nonetheless, they managed to finish the dance and were rewarded by a warm round of applause by the attendees.

At that point a guide, the bastonero, organized the order and position of the couples that took to the floor and led them in a series of dances, mainly contradanzas and habaneras, forming them in lines, circles, quartets, trios, and duets. The dances became more and more animated, helped perhaps by the saoco (rum and coconut milk) cocktails that were continuously being distributed to both the couples on the floor and the spectators.

Rino and Rodolfito had remained out of sight most of the evening but, as alcohol began coursing through their veins, they became less inhibited and joined the dancers in an habanera and stayed on the floor thereafter. There were murmurs of disapproval and Cecilia pursed her lips, trying to decide whether to intervene and disrupt the proceedings. She hesitated and let matters go on.

The next number played by the orchestra was a danza, *El Sungambelo*, which was well-known throughout Cuba. It was a favorite of Carmela and Alberto, who had danced it together many times. As they were starting to dance, Rodolfito walked over, tapped Alberto on the shoulder, and offered his arm to the surprised Carmela.

The danza had a particular feature: the male held his female partner in a closed dance position, later adopted by the waltz. This holding position between the partners allowed a greater degree of intimacy than was afforded by dances in which the partners did not touch. Thus, Rodolfito's move was quite daring. Alberto grimaced and stepped aside, leaving Rodolfito and Carmela moving to the slow, sensuous rhythm of the music.

"You are the most excellent woman I ever laid eyes on!" whispered Rodolfito, his voice a bit slurred by alcohol.

"You are drunk … and you stink!" replied Carmela, teetering between indignation and amusement.

"My dear, what you smell is bay rum cologne, I spent half my salary on a bottle hoping to meet some beauty, and by Saint Anne I did!" he replied, squeezing her shoulder.

"You are lying" she replied, suppressing a smile. "You just have been drinking my uncle's saoco."

"I may have had a sip or two, but if I am drunk, it is because the sight of you has made me lose my senses."

As they continued to gyrate, other couples moved back so that, in a few moments, they were alone in the center of the room. "Let go of me! Everyone is watching us!" protested Carmela.

"I'll never let you go. I…" started Rodolfito before he was yanked away from the girl by a extremely upset Leonardo. "Get your hands of my niece, you filthy bum!" he shouted, seizing Rodolfito by the neck and starting to drag him towards the front door.

"Hey, don't touch my brother!" screamed Rino, who had been watching the proceedings with amusement that turned to alarm. Rino tried to free Rodolfito from Leonardo's grasp, who turned around and punched Rino hard on the face, dropping him to the floor.

Pandemonium erupted. Several people moved to restrain Leonardo, who had released Rodolfito and hovered above Rino, who was sitting on the ground nursing a broken nose. Leonardo pointed the finger at Rino and ordered: "Both of you, get out of here right now before I call the alguacil and have you thrown in jail!"

Rino got to his feet sullenly and headed for the door, murder in his eyes. He was joined by Rodolfito, who in the meantime had pleaded with Carmela in a low voice: "Can I please see you again? Please! Please!?"

Startled, Carmela moved her head up and down once.

Chapter 3

Pilón, June, 1859: Aftermath

Thou wast the prettiest babe that e'er I nursed
An I might live to see thee married once
Nurse, Romeo and Juliet, Act IV, Scene 3

Cecilia had never seen her brother-in-law so angry. She knew Leonardo had a temper, but most of the time he kept it under control. Obviously, he was upset that Carmela's party, on which he had invested a lot of money, had been ruined by the incident with those ruffians, and his reputation as an amiable businessman had been impaired.

When the last remaining guests had departed, Leonardo got the family together in the empty city hall and vented his frustration. "How did those *negros sucios* get the notion that they could get away with crashing our party?" He let out an angry sigh. "It was my fault, I guess, for not posting a couple of guys at the door to make sure that only our guests could come in…"

Alberto kept his eyes lowered, debating whether to fess up and reveal his part in the fiasco. He decided he had to come clean for Carmela's sake. "Er… I know those guys from playing football around town…" He paused for a second to gather his courage: "I may have told them it would be fine for them to show up and have some cake…"

"You, imbecile!" exploded Leonardo. "I should take it off your hide!" He started in the boy's direction, but Cecilia moved between them. "What is done is done. Nobody could have predicted what happened." She put her arm protectively around his son.

"Anyway, it was a very nice party, and I enjoyed myself a lot" cut in Carmela.

Later, Carmela questioned her brother: "Who were those fellows you invited to my party?"

"I dunno, I play football with them and other guys on weekends on the lot behind the church."

"You invited them, and you don't know anything about them?"

"Well, I know that Rodolfito, the one who danced with you, is an apprentice at Galván's blacksmith shop. I don't think his brother Rino works anywhere."

"Where do they live?"

"In a shack at the edge of town. They are very poor."

"Also quite brazen. Where did that Rodolfito get the notion that I would want to have anything to do with him?"

Graciela, who was overhearing the conversation, cut in: "Maybe he has read *Romeo y Julieta*."

"I don't think so. I am pretty sure he and his brother have no schooling, though the parish priest taught them to read and write" replied Alberto. "Anyhow, he was surely acting out of character being so forward with Carmela. He is usually quiet and well-behaved. Not at all like Rino."

"He was probably blinded by my beauty" chuckled Carmela.

"Alcohol makes us do the weirdest things" replied Graciela, not trying to hide a smile.

Chapter 4

Pilón, June, 1859: Getting to the Church on Time

> *I got to get there in the morning*
> *Spruced up and lookin' in my prime*
> Alan Jay Lerner, My Fair Lady

Rodolfo was burning with desire to lay eyes again on the beautiful Carmela Serrano. The girl had silently consented to their meeting but getting it to happen was nearly impossible. Showing up at the Serrano manor house was out to question: in the aftermath of the party Leonardo had bought a fierce mastiff whose menacing barks could be heard two blocks away and posted an armed watchman to keep undesirables from disturbing the family. Rodolfo had known that Carmela left the house to attend her sewing club meetings in the company of her mother and Yaya, but Rodolfo had no female relatives or friends who were members of the club and could serve as go-betweens.

But there was the church. The women in the Serrano household attended services at the parish church, a two-room structure located only a few blocks from the manor house. If the weather was good, the four women went on foot to the mid-morning masses on Sundays and holidays. Leonardo was too busy, he claimed, to accompany them except on special occasions, and had felt no need to send Ruperto or some other of his servants or employees to escort them.

"If I could only set Carmela aside for five minutes, I would be able to make my case and try to win her heart" lamented Rodolfo to his brother.

"And you want me to help you get some alone time with your sweetie" replied Rino, sarcasm dripping from his voice.

"I don't see how you could manage that" replied Rodolfo.

"Oh, I think I could manage that. The question is whether I want to do it."

"Oh, come on Rino, don't play with me. You

know how important this is."

Rino remained silent for a few moments. "All right, I will do it for you, seeing that you are my favorite brother. When do you want to do it?"

"Next time they will go to church is Sunday morning, for the nine o'clock mass. Say some time before nine?"

"Fine. This is what we will do."

***

At twenty minutes to nine, Cecilia, her daughters, and Yaya emerged from the street that led to the parochial church, walking by a vacant lot adjacent to the church. As they did, Rodolfo – who was stationed behind the church – waved his arms widely, signaling for a gaggle of teenagers led by Rino to enter the vacant lot. The boys split into two camps and started screaming at each other. What appeared to be a vicious fight broke out and someone started overturning trash receptacles and setting them on fire.

Cecilia shouted in a quivering voice: "Let's run into the church! Quick!" She was, as usual, the leader of the group and soon entered the church with Graciela close on her heels. At that point, Rodolfo emerged from hiding, seized Carmela by the arm, and dragged her behind the building while at the same time motioning to Yaya to join them.

"Carmela, I am desperately in love with you and must see you. Please meet with me soon so we can talk, or I will kill myself!" There was utter desperation in his voice and Carmela hesitated a moment.

"You are out of your mind! But don't do anything rash! I don't want to have that on my conscience."

"I swear that I will!"

Carmela stared at the boy intently. He was a handsome, tall, strong looking youth of mixed race like her. He did not seem in any way threatening, and she felt flattered by his attention. "All right. Yaya goes to the market Monday mornings to get fresh produce for the family. I will send a note for you with her. Now let me go, before my mother comes out looking for me!"

"Thank you, my love!" replied Rodolfo, letting go and disappearing behind the church.

"That boy is crazy as a goat!" declared Yaya, rolling her eyes.

"I know, but don't tell mama what just happened!" warned Carmela.

"I won't. But you take care, you hear!" replied the slave, giving her ward a sly look.

Chapter 5

Pilón, June, 1859: Brief Encounter

Every sunset brings the promise of a new dawn.
Ralph Waldo Emerson

They met at sunset at the main Pilón dock, a concrete structure with an ironwork extension that allowed small and medium sized craft to drop anchor and bring on or unload merchandise. Deserted at this late hour, it sat totally in the open, visible from the nearby sugar mill and manor house. It held a wooden shack where port officials had their office. Carmela had secured a key to the shack and waited inside while Yaya, shivering in the evening breeze, stood guard outside.

They had to wait only a few minutes before a figure emerged from the shadows. It was Rodolfo, wearing work clothes: cotton pants, a tattered shirt, a straw hat, and a heavy leather apron. His first words were an apology for his dress: "I could not get away from the shop until just now. Galván is busy these days."

"Never mind that" replied Carmela. "What is it that you must talk to me about, Rodolfito?"

"Oh." He was a bit deflated by the girl's tart tone but recovered. "Carmela, please call me Rodolfo from now on. I have aged from thinking about you since your party. I love you!"

"How can you say you love me? We have barely met, and not under the best circumstances."

"I know. I'm sorry for my behavior and my brother's. But see, the moment you entered that room, dressed all in white like an angel from heaven, I felt like my life was changed. I want to live with you, or not at all!"

"That is ludicrous. I'm just an ordinary girl. What's there about me that you find so attractive?"

"I can't describe it. The way you move. How you carry yourself. Your smile…"

"I am no beauty. There must be many girls in this town that are better looking than I."

"I have met the other girls. None can compare

with you."

"How old are you?"

"I'll be seventeen this December."

"I just turned fifteen. Don't you think you are too young to be serious about me? Won't you change your mind in a week or year?"

"I know my heart. My feelings won't change."

"Well, supposing you are right. How about me? I don't feel any attraction for you."

"I think you are mistaken. I noticed how you looked at me when we were dancing. You may not love me yet, but you are at least interested."

"I sort of admired your daring, but that does not mean I feel anything for you."

"Well, at least you don't hate me for ruining your party. That is a good start."

Carmela could not help breaking into a small smile. "No, I don't *hate* you but…"

The boy did not let her finish. "Well, that's a start! I would hope we can at least be friends."

"I don't know. We are so different. I don't think we have much in common."

"Not true. We are both young, smart, and have a good heart. What else do we need to become friends?"

"You make it sound like it would be a simple matter. For one thing, my family surely would not approve of our being friends. How would we meet? Where? What would we do? You work and I study and have my own social life, and the two do not seem to be compatible."

"Those are details that can be worked out. All I ask is that you give us a chance to get to know each other better."

There was a long silence. For the first time, Carmela stared intently at Rodolfo, whose face was contorted with anxiety. He had fine features and, except for his kinky hair, could have passed for White. Overall, he was handsome and appeared honest and sincere. The social life opportunities in this backwater were not that great and returning to La Habana was not an immediate prospect. Perhaps this eager boy would prove good company, if it could be arranged without upsetting matters with the rest of the family.

"Well, I am willing to give friendship a try, but you should have absolutely no illusions of anything else. You can send me word with Yaya as to how you want to proceed. And remember, I don't want to get in trouble with my relatives."

Chapter 6

Pilón, June, 1859: Meeting at the Market

> *Thou wast the prettiest babe that e'er I nursed*
> *An I might live to see thee married once*
> Nurse, Romeo and Juliet, Act IV, Scene 3

Yaya, usually quite placid, became agitated and began gesticulating angrily. "Are you out of your mind? Take the missy to *El Malecón*? To hang out with the criminals and the drunks and the putas? Not in your life!"

Rino tried to calm the slave, whose explosion had caused heads to turn all around them in the market. "No, señora, it's not like that. Me and my bro wouldn't dream of having your pretty miss mingle with the riff-raff. Listen, we have it all figured out."

It took a while before the slave's volcanic eruption abated to the point Rino could go on with his explanation. "See, me and Rodolfito are friends with Luciano, the owner of the bar and have cut a deal with him."

"A deal?" asked the black woman suspiciously.

"Yeah. See, you will bring Carmelita through the back entrance and walk a few steps until you hit the bar's back room, where Luciano stores the liquor. I will have a table and chairs set up there. Your miss and my brother will sit in complete privacy, and none'll know they are there."

"I don't like it" insisted Yaya. "If Carmelita is seen there with your brother, her reputation will be ruined. And for what?" Her voice was rising again, and Rino hastened to stem the flow of angry words. "Nobody will, Yaya. I and my friends will stand guard in front and rear of the bar to block anyone from getting in."

"I'm not telling the miss about this crazy scheme of yours."

"Come on, Yaya" said Rino placatingly. "Carmelita is waiting for word from us. Let her make her own decisions. You tell her, or I will need to tell her myself."

The slave was scared by the possibility of Carmela being approached by the ruffian. "No, no. I'll tell her" she declared.

"But she will laugh at the idea. She's a very sensible girl, although a little bit impulsive at times," thought the servant.

Carmela, however, did not laugh at the proposition. It was a wild and dangerous plan, but at least it meant that Rodolfito was serious about her. She felt flattered and somewhat excited by the opportunity to do something rebellious and a little naughty that broke the dull routine of her life in Pilón.

"Next time you see either brother at the market, get exact details so we can plan for the meeting. I will do this once, and then never again."

Chapter 7

Pilón, June, 1859: In the Backroom

Many a time from a bad beginning great friendships
have sprung up.
Terence

The atmosphere was tense as Rino escorted the women to the small room in the back of the bar and withdrew to stand guard by the back door. Yaya, who was accompanying her ward, sat on a stool against the wall, ready to snap in defense of Carmela if the situation warranted it. She was sweating profusely, in part from the stifling summer heat that filled the room, but mostly from nerves. Bringing the young girl to this den of perdition was the hardest chore she had ever had to perform, and she was expecting that something dreadful would happen at any moment.

Shortly after Carmela took a seat on one side of the small table, Rodolfo entered through the bar side and sat across from her. "Thank you for agreeing to meet me here. It means the world to me."

"I have thought about it and decided we cannot be friends because we move in different circles, and you and your brother already have had a bad start with our family."

"I don't think our start was all that bad. You seemed to enjoy dancing with me. But put that aside. Do you find me ugly or repulsive?"

Carmela felt she had to shake her head in denial. "No, I don't."

"Have I offended you in any way? Do I look like a criminal, or put you in fear for your safety?" Carmela uttered a silent negation.

"So, what's the harm in us sitting together having a nice conversation every now and then?"

Carmela sighed.

"Good. Let me tell you about myself. I'm not from these parts. My parents lived in a *palenque* east of here; my father was killed when the Spanish government raided their settlement eight years ago, but my mother, brother, and I escaped and came to

Pilón. We were given shelter in this parish church and my mother was hired as a laundress for the church. She had a bad heart and died two years ago. Since then, Rino and I have been on our own, living in a shack the church gave to our mother. Father Pastor has looked after us from a distance and has taught us to read and write. As you know, I am an apprentice to Galván, the town's blacksmith; Rino does what odd jobs he can. We are poor but honest."

"How about your grandparents?"

"I never learned about my father's ancestors, only that he was an escaped slave. My grandmother on my mother's side came to Cuba sixty years ago when the troubles started in Haiti and her owner, along with his family and slaves, had to escape to Cuba. My father met my mother in Santiago and talked her into going to the palenque with him. How about your family?"

"My grandfather on my father's side had a very interesting life and left behind an account of his travels. He was of mixed race: Black, White, and maybe even Indian. He made a fortune from selling for a health spa resort a farm he had bought near La Habana, and married grandmother Graciela when he was in his forties. He had two boys, my father now dead and Uncle Leonardo, who became a financier and increased our property holdings. Mother is from a poor family in a small town near La Habana, nothing special about them."

"So, we are not that different, are we?"

"I guess not," allowed Carmela.

***

Carmela had to shake Yaya awake; the slave had fallen asleep, her head resting against the wall and her mouth whistling with a soft snore. Yaya became immediately alert and gasped in alarm. "Are you safe? What did that boy do to ye?" she screeched.

"Nothing, Yaya. He's a good boy" replied Carmela reassuringly.

"What time is it?" asked Yaya, rubbing sleep from her eyes.

"It's getting late. Let's go home before night falls."

"How long was I asleep?"

"At least an hour" smiled Rodolfo, getting up to stand next to the women.

"Oh, Changó bendito, I should be whipped. What happened?" she asked again, suspiciously.

"We just talked. I'll tell you on the way home. Now we must go."

The slave got to her feet slowly, wincing from the effort.

"When will I see you again?" ventured the boy, wistfully.

"I don't know. Let me figure it out. I'll send word with Yaya."

Rodolfo let out a sigh of relief. "Alright. I hope it is soon."

"Greedy boy" smiled Carmela, heading for the back door, followed by her slave.

Chapter 8

Pilón, June - July, 1859: Behind the Church

We kiss in a shadow, we hide from the moon,
Our meetings are few, and over too soon.
Rodgers and Hammerstein, The King and I

The routine was set quickly: Every Friday night at 8 pm a number of devout ladies would gather at the parish church to pray a novena, which in the month of June was addressed to Saint Anthony of Padua, the saint who supposedly helped find lost things or mend affairs gone off-kilter. Carmela would leave home early "to engage in her own private prayer," inviting her mother and Graciela to join her; she knew full well that neither would be interested in such devotions and would stay home.

Yaya and Carmela would arrive shortly before seven and, instead of entering the church, would proceed to a small garden to the side of the building. Carmela would sit on a bench in the garden, Yaya standing guard in front of her to provide cover and warn of possible intruders. Rodolfo would arrive at seven o'clock sharp and sit next to the girl. They would chat amiably until almost eight, and when Yaya alerted them that other women were approaching, the couple would stand. Rodolfo would kiss her hand and disappear while Carmela would enter the church and pray to Saint Anthony for help of retrieving whatever she might have lost.

In time, their conversations became more intimate, their whispered voices turned more tender, until at the end of the third weekly meeting, Rodolfo kissed Carmela on the cheek and caressed her bare arm, sending a chill down her spine. Yaya, watching the proceedings with mounting concern, grabbed her mistress and whisked her away, casting an angry look at the daring young man. "That boy will be your ruin!" she hissed as she dragged Carmela inside the church.

***

Carmela's mode of attending the novenas was unlike those of the other ladies that showed up at the prayer meetings. Instead of entering with a bowed head and seeking to join the other attendees as they gathered before the altar, she rushed to the back row and sat alone, silently looking at the ceiling while the priest led the faithful in their prayers. An attentive observer could only conclude that the girl was marking time while the devotions ran their course.

It was not long before her behavior was noted by the ladies and became the subject of gossip among the village women, one of whom – a friend of Cecilia – referred obliquely to the peculiar praying habits of the youngest of the Serranos during the next sewing club meeting. She did not claim that there was anything wrong with Carmela's behavior, but the girl "seemed to be consumed by some private concern that was unusual for anyone so young and of such a good family."

Cecilia questioned her daughter sternly, suspecting some romantic entanglement, but Carmela was adamant in her denials. Yet the girl didn't sound sincere. So, Cecilia pressed Yaya for answers. "You are supposed to be looking after Carmela's well-being and don't seem to be doing too good a job at it," she charged the slave. At first,

Yaya denied that there was anything irregular about Carmela's behavior, but when Cecilia posed the direct question "She's seeing a boy, isn't she?" Yaya could not continue covering up for her ward. "It's nothing like that…" she started, but Cecilia cut her off: "Who's he?" Yaya stammered something unintelligible, so Cecilia pressed: "The name, Yaya! Tell me his name!"

"It's Rodolfito, the boy who danced with her with at her quince."

Cecilia remained silent for a moment, stunned, and then exploded: "That ruffian? What has he done to my daughter? Have you have let him be alone with Carmela?!"

"Miss Cecilia, nuthin' has happened, as Holy Mary is my witness!" She stopped for a second to catch her breath and continued: "They sit outside the church for a few minutes on Friday nights, just before the novena, and chat! Nuthin' else!"

"How long has his going on?"

"Three or four weeks, I swear!"

"I have a mind to have Leonardo put you up for sale at the next market in Manzanillo!"

"Please, miss, nuthin' has happened!"

"Nothing, eh?" barked Cecilia. "My daughter's honor compromised! And with a common delinquent, a good for nothing vagrant off the streets! I'll have you whipped!"

"Miss, please punish me all you want, but do nuthin' to Carmelita, she's a good girl and has done nuthin' wrong, I swear!!"

Cecilia raised her arm to strike the slave but held herself in check. "I'll be the judge of that! Give me the details and tell me everything!"

***

Later that day, Cecilia had a tense confrontation with her daughter.

"You lied to me, and worse yet, you are hanging out with that scum! What were you thinking?!"

"Rodolfo is no scum, but a very decent man, and I like him a lot."

"He and his brother ruined the party we put so much effort into setting up for you! How can you be friends with him after that?!"

"Well, I'm sorry about the party, but it was not his fault. If Uncle Leonardo had not gotten so worked up, everything would have been fine!"

"And you still defend him! What has gotten into you?!"

"Nothing, mother! He's nice and smart and treats me like a grownup, which is more than you and Uncle do around here!"

"Well, I forbid you to see him again!"

"I'm old enough to decide who to see."

"I said and I meant it! Stop meeting that Rodolfito, or else…"

"What? Besides keeping me a prisoner in this dump, what else can you do to me?"

"You'll see…"

Chapter 9

Pilón, July, 1859: Confrontation

I didn't want anybody seeing my fire until I burned them with it.

Cameron Conaway

After her temper subsided, Cecilia examined her options and realized there were few. It was her fault that her children were confined to this backwater with no opportunities to make connections with people of any social significance. Carmela did not have much to choose from, after all. She had to take her children back to La Habana.

But, for the moment, she needed to make sure her daughter did not ruin her life by having an affair with someone from the gutter. She had to nip this romance in the bud.

She was reluctant to get her brother-in-law involved in this mess, but she knew Carmela. She was impulsive and stubborn as a mule. Punishing her would not work. They had to pull this weed from its roots.

"You are not going to believe this" she said to Leonardo, barging into his sugar mill office as he was ill-humoredly going through some bills. "What now?" he asked with some asperity.

"That boy that crashed our party for Carmela and created that big mess is bothering my daughter again."

Leonardo dropped the papers he was reading and gave a startled look to his sister-in-law. "Bothering how?"

"I don't know, stalking her on the way to church, trying to draw her into conversation. He apparently has not given up on her."

"The bastard!" Leonardo got up from his chair abruptly, causing it to tumble to the floor. "Don't worry, sister. Leave it up to me. I'll have a chat with the squirt!"

***

At dawn the following day, Leonardo and two of his bodyguards descended on a one-room shack at the edge of town near the foot of the mountains. Instead of knocking on the door, Leonardo yelled angrily: "Come out, cabrones, we want to talk to you!"

There was no response, and Leonardo directed his men: "Break the damn door down!" With savage kicks, the men tore the door off its hinges and sent it tumbling into the humble dwelling.

Rodolfito was not there. Rino, freshly awoken from sleep, stood against the back wall, waving a cattle branding iron, a scowl on his face. "Come on, hijos de la gran puta, come and get it!"

Neither Leonardo nor his men were armed and, instead of entering the shack, stood at the doorway. Leonardo questioned the boy angrily: "Where is your brother?"

"None of your goddamn business!" spat back Rino. Then he added: "He's at work."

"Tell him that if I hear again that he has been bothering my niece Carmela, I'll break every bone in his body, and yours, too!"

"Why don't you try that now. I'm here waiting for you!"

"Naw, we'll be back" replied Leonardo, waving his men away.

"You are goddamn cowards, and I'll take on any one of you mano a mano, any day you dare come by!" were Rino's parting words.

Leonardo glowered but turned his back on the shack and filed away with his men.

***

Late that night, unidentified persons threw burning, rum-soaked rags at the shack, whose palm-frond roof immediately caught fire. The shack burned to the ground in only a few minutes.

Rodolfo was able to get out with only minor burns. Rino was slow getting up from his slumber and was severely burned.

Chapter 10

Pilón, July, 1859: Convalescence

That which does not kill us makes us stronger.
Friedrich Nietzsche

Rino would have died had it not been for the intervention of Arturo Galván, the blacksmith for whom Rodolfo worked. Galván took it upon himself to transport Rodolfo and a delirious Rino to Pilón's tiny urgent care cottage at the edge of town run by the Sisters of Charity. There, the three nuns in charge of the facility gave their full attention to the burned boy and his grieving brother.

Sister Simona, who ran the facility, developed

an instant liking for Rodolfo and, after the first couple of days, delicately broached the subject of the boys' future. "You should not have been by yourselves to start with. I can help place you and your brother, once he recovers, in an orphanage in Santiago."

Rodolfo reacted strongly to the suggestion. "Sister, we'll be eternally grateful to you and Sisters Alina and María de los Angeles for the care you have given us, but I'd rather die than lose my freedom, and I am sure Rino feels the same way. I already have an occupation and would very much like to continue to ply my trade as a blacksmith in this area."

"It would be very irregular for us to assist two minors to remain outside the bounds of the law; you belong in an orphanage, at least for the next couple of years."

"Sister, you would undo the great help you have given us by confining us to a place where we don't belong. We've been functioning in the world for the last two years and can't be considered children in need of care anymore. If those criminals had not set our home afire, we would still be managing rather well here in Pilón."

Sister Simona remained silent for a long while. Finally, she chose what she felt was the safest course of action.

"We have been working at this clinic only a short time and are not familiar with the general population of this area. Sister Alina, however, is from the Manzanillo area north of here and may know of a family there that would be willing to accept you two as their wards for the next couple of years. I will seek her counsel."

"But Sister…"

"We'll take this up again a bit later. In the meantime, go visit with your brother. He can use the company."

***

That afternoon, Sister Simona came to the room where Rodolfo was sitting next to the pallet where Rino rested. As she entered, she could hear the wounded boy's agitated voice: "I tell you I'll kill that bastard Serrano! With my own hands! He'll have to pay for this!"

"Shh…" cautioned Sister Simona. "No such words may be uttered in the place dedicated to Our Lord. Hush."

"Look at my face!" demanded Rino. "I bet I will have scars the rest of my life!"

"Talk about taking another man's life is not

Christian. If you did that, it would be more than your face that would burn in Hell!"

Rino was about to utter a retort, but the nun continued: "Hush. Sister Alina here has an idea that might solve your problem, at least for the short run."

Sister Alina, a demure young woman, approached the pallet and spoke to both youths: "My uncle Manolo owns a small farm on the banks of the river Yara, not far from Manzanillo. I can write him and ask whether he would be willing to employ two young men as farmhands and serve as their guardian. Would you like me to do that?"

"How long would it take to hear back from your uncle?" asked Sister Simona.

"We send a rider to get our post to Manzanillo twice a week, coming back the following day. I could ask Carlos to make a side trip to Yara and get word from my uncle the same day. So, we would have the answer in three or four days."

"Please write to your uncle tonight. We will send the letter with Carlos tomorrow and have the answer by the end of the week" ordered Sister Simona. Anticipating an objection from one or both brothers, she added "you boys can't turn down an offer until you get it. Plus, you are going nowhere in the next few days anyways."

***

The answer came back in the form of a letter from Sister Alina's aunt: "Dear Alina: Your uncle is busy finishing the spring harvest and is not much of a writer, so I'm responding to your letter on his behalf as well as mine. This house is empty since our son left us to serve in the Spanish army. We would not mind having some young faces around to brighten our days. The work is hard, and we can't pay much, but we would welcome those two unfortunate children to come live with us and stay as long as they need. Please warn them that we are humble people and so is our home, but they will always have a good sancocho for dinner at the end of the day. Please send word back to us whether they will be coming and, if so, when. May our Lady of Charity bless with you and keep you in good health. Love, Your Aunt Isabel."

***

"I'm not doing that" was Rino's emphatic response to the proposal. We are not guajiros, our life is in this town, not on a sitio like former slaves. Plus, I have a score to settle in Pilón and am not moving anywhere until I'm done."

Rodolfo's feelings were very much the same, but he had a practical side that helped him consider the situation they faced. "Listen, I don't like the idea any more than you do, but we are in a bind. You need to get better and recover your strength, and we need to plan how we are going to get our lives back. I say we go to that farm for a few weeks and then we'll see."

The decision was made for them through a visit from Sister Simona the following day. She went right down to the point: "Listen, boys, we need for you to move on. As you know, this is a small facility, and we have other sick people requiring attention. Rino is sufficiently recovered from the worst of his burns to be able to get out of here. What are you going to do about the offer from Sister Alina's family?"

Rodolfo responded: "Are you trying to get rid of us?"

The nun blushed slightly. "It's not that. I don't feel you are safe around here. Whoever carried out this terrible crime may not stop and may come back to finish you off."

"Mother…" started Rino, but his brother cut in: "Sister, we are grateful for the offer, and we are inclined to accept it."

"I'll have Carlos deliver word when he goes to Manzanillo tomorrow. We'll borrow a cart, and he can drive you both to Yara once he comes back."

***

While they waited for Carlos to return, Rodolfo went to see Sister Simona. "Sister, I must ask you for a big favor. I need to deliver a letter for me."

"To whom?"

"The letter is to be delivered to Yaya, the cook for the Serrano family."

"You are writing an old slave a letter?"

"It's not for her… but someone else."

"I see. Why don't you deliver it yourself?"

"You've said it before. I will be in danger if I show my face in public in this town."

"Still, we should not get involved in your affairs, which I suspect are rather dubious."

"Sister, I beg you! I agreed to go to Yara and talked my brother into doing the same, but I can't leave without sending a farewell letter to someone."

"That's even worse. Are you trying to make me into a procuress, a vulgar Celestina? Have you no shame?"

Rodolfito broke up in tears. "Sister Simona, there is nothing illicit in the letter I am writing.

62

You can even read it yourself to decide whether to deliver it. But please, I have nobody else to whom I can turn."

"Still, I don't think it is right for us to be involved."

"Well, I will have to do it myself then. I will go to the market tomorrow and hand it to Yaya. If something happens to me, it will be on your conscience!"

"Alright. Write the letter and show it to me. If I think it is prudent to do so, I will have Sister Maria de los Angeles take it to market tomorrow and hand it to that Yaya, if she can be found."

***

"My much-esteemed Carmela,

Due to circumstances of which you are aware, my brother and I must leave Pilón for some time. I don't know when I will be able to return, but rest assured that I will be back, and that I hope to resume our friendship at that point. Please think of me as well as you can. I will always carry your memory in my heart.

Matias Travieso-Diaz

Until next we see each other, be well.

Affectionately,
Your servant,
Rodolfo Durán"

Chapter 11

Yara, July - August, 1859: A new Life

Coarse rice to eat, water to drink, my bent arm for a pillow - therein is happiness.

Confucius

Life was hard in *Los Suspiros*, the farm owned by the Galáns in Yara at the foot of the mountains. Manuel ("Manolo") and his wife Isabel worked from before dawn to after dusk attending to crops, raising pigs and goats, getting products ready for the market, and attending to the thousand chores that are required day to day in a small farming operation like theirs. They had two male slaves who assisted with the toughest jobs such as clearing the woods, cutting the cane in the plot devoted to support sugar production, and tilling the fields, but the owner had to do everything else.

Coffee beans were the farm's main crop. The ripe cherries had to be plucked from the branches of the coffee trees, often requiring workers to clear the area surrounding the trees and then reaching up; the repeated operation often caused muscle strains, particularly for those–like Rodolfo and Rino–who had not performed such work before. Spending hours in the sun was exhausting and left the cortadores tired and irritable. Rodolfo was used to working hard before, but blacksmithing indoors was entirely different from outdoor labor on a farm.

The brothers reacted in different ways to the demands of living as fugitives in an isolated sitio. Rodolfo, ever polite, did his best to ingratiate himself with those that had offered him shelter. Isabel was taken with the boy, whose dark looks reminded her of her faraway son, and soon was treating him like another member of the family. Rino, on the other hand, was standoffish and barely civil to the Galáns, and made no effort to hide his anger and the pain at the burns that covered his face and much of his body. Only the influence of

Rodolfo's exemplary behavior, plus Isabel's pity at his condition, saved him from being shown the door.

Matters came to a head four weeks after their arrival in Yara. It was a hot, humid August morning that promised to be a scorcher. As they finished their breakfast, Manolo announced: "We need to move harvesting to the area at the eastern edge of the property, for the cherries there were close to ready for picking yesterday and should be gathered today before they spoil."

Rodolfo said nothing, but Rino voiced a loud protest: "That sucks! That hillside is steep and hasn't been cleared by Domingo and Eusebio, so we'll spend the day like lumberjacks and will catch heatstroke. No way!"

Manolo gave him an icy stare and replied: "I think you are recovered enough to at least do some berry picking. You *will* go work on that hill…"

As they were about to take off, Manolo drew Rodolfo aside: "Un momento, Rodolfito."

Rodolfo knew what was coming and sighed.

"Rodolfito, you know we are fond of you and happy to have you with us. But your brother has a very bad attitude, and I have a mind to send him packing, so you better have a word with him. He needs to change his ways."

"Don Manuel, you know how grateful we are for your giving us shelter in our difficult situation. Things have been tough on Rino, and he can't get over the injustice of being the victim of a terrible injury and on top of that, being driven out of town. I'll speak to him tonight."

The promised talk never took place, however. The day's work on the new hill was truly exhausting, and by the time the boys came back from the field they were dripping with sweat, their faces red like ripe mangoes. They had a quick dinner and collapsed on their cots.

Shortly before dawn, something disturbed Rodolfo, who tossed and turned for a few moments but finally sat up, rubbing sleep of his eyes. As he looked around the room, his brother's cot was empty.

"That jerk ran away with our mule" bellowed Manuel a bit later. "And he took all the food Isabel had left in the pantry, and my shotgun! Desgraciado!"

Chapter 12

Manzanillo, August, 1859: Impatience

*Anxiety does not empty tomorrow of its sorrows, but only
empties today of its strength.*
Charles Spurgeon

Manolo announced he was driving his cart to
Manzanillo to report the theft of his mule and
shotgun to the local alguacil. "If that crazy boy
commits a crime using my gun, I don't want the
blame to fall on my shoulders. Plus, I want my
mule and weapon back!"

"Could I please ride with you?" begged
Rodolfo. "I must get back to Pilón to catch my
brother before he does something really bad."

Manolo obliged. "Take your things with you. You'll always be welcome at our house, but I don't want to see your brother ever again."

"I'm so sorry…" began Rodolfo, but he could not go on. His eyes welled with tears.

***

They arrived in Manzanillo in the early afternoon, and Rodolfo stationed himself outside the feed store, which also served as mail center for the area. He was hoping to find someone who was willing to take him down to Pilón in exchange for a few coins that a tearful Isabel had given him as he left Yara. There were no takers; the closest anyone would be able to take him was Niquero, another small town about a five day walk from Pilón. He had no money to buy a mule or a donkey, if one could be found for sale in Niquero, and his need was too urgent to attempt traveling on foot.

Sunset was drawing near, and Rodolfo's desperation was increasing when a familiar sight caught his eye: Carlos' cart, drawn by Raquel the nag, was plodding its way up the road north from Niquero.

Rodolfo began waiving wildly at the approaching vehicle, which eventually stopped right in front of him. Carlos dismounted and greeted the boy:

"Hey, Rodolfito! What you doin here?"

"Hi, Carlos. I'm so happy to see you!" Without further explanation, Rodolfo blurted: "You must take me back to Pilón right away!"

"Well, I migh do dat, if you are really nice to me." The black man smiled broadly and went on: "But it'll be tomorrow, after I pick up the mail for the Sisters and run some errands."

"Can those things wait a couple of days? I've got a real emergency!"

"No, mah boy. For one thing, I'm plumb tired and need to get some rest before heading back, and so does poor Raquel. I also need to get them some medications fixed for the cottage, and dat will take time. Sister Simona would skin me alive if I showed up without them medications."

"Oh, God, I really need to go right now…!"

"What's dem rush?"

"It's my brother Rino. He's off to Pilón himself, and is up to no good!"

"I sorry to hear dat. But the best I can do is rush back in the morning."

Rodolfo began biting his knuckles but finally relented: "Alright. We'll go back early tomorrow. It's all in God's hands!"

Chapter 13

Pilón, August, 1859: All Hell Has Broken Loose

Pride and excess bring disaster for man.
Xun Kuang

The nuns at the urgent care cottage were a bit alarmed when Raquel brought the cart down the muddy street at an unusually fast pace for an old nag. The animal was panting loudly from prolonged exertion.

The trip normally took about ten hours over the unreliable road (a dirt track that often turned quite muddy) and Carlos typically drove back from Manzanillo after breakfast, so he normally arrived in Pilón after sunset. Yet it was barely merienda time, mid-afternoon. Something strange was going on.

As the cart arrived, the nuns noticed that Carlos was not traveling alone. Next to him on the bench was Rodolfo Durán. "What is he doing here?" asked Sister Simona to no one in particular. "We went to a lot of trouble to get them out of town to protect them!"

She was about to ask the same question to Rodolfo when he anticipated her:

"Sister Simona, I need your help. My brother has gone crazy and came down here armed with a shotgun. I'm afraid he's gona do something terrible!"

The nun turned pale and stood silent for a moment. Then her face set in a rigid mask. "Do you have any idea where he may be headed?"

"My guess is that he is gone to the sugar mill's manor house. He's convinced that Leonardo Serrano is behind the attack that left him all burnt up. He may be seeking revenge against Serrano."

Sister Simona's reaction was frenzied: "You need to stay here with us until things get sorted out. If you are out on the street, you may get arrested or hurt. I will send word to the alguacil. Carlos, go out right now to the police station and tell Alvarez that we have gotten word that Rinaldo Durán, the kid whose house got burned last month, is back in town, is armed, and may be going around the manor house. Don't mention that his brother is also in town."

Without a word, Carlos turned around, jumped back on the cart, and yanked on Raquel's reins to get the horse moving again to the equine's discomfort.

***

Even before he approached the manor house, Carlos noticed that trouble was brewing. Half of the town's inhabitants were on the streets, milling around and talking loudly with one another. Carlos caught snippets of the conversations:

"Did they catch him?"

"They say he is hiding in the woods!"

"How is Don Leonardo?"

"It's so awful! And Ruperto had three small children! What is poor Eulalia going to do?"

Carlos could not reach the mill's gate because an excited mob was gathered in front of it. He got off Raquel and asked to no one in particular: "What happened here?" There were several overlapping answers, but after a while he was able to discern that at dawn, someone had entered the mill compound through the open gate, marched to the manor house, shot Rupert as he stood guard at the front door, and fired through the dining room glass window at the Serrano family having breakfast, striking both Cecilia and Leonardo. She had sustained only a shoulder wound, but a bullet hit Leonardo in the stomach, and he was in serious condition. A startled Albertico had identified a fleeing Rinaldo Durán as the marksman.

Carlos wasted no time in further investigations. He got back in the cart and hastily returned to the urgent care cottage, finding all three nuns and Rodolfo standing outside, clearly waiting for him. "I'm sorry, Sor Rosario, I didn't get to warn Alvarez because there was no need." Facing Rodolfo, Carlos continued accusingly: "Your brother shot the Serranos and is on the lam!"

Sister Simona replied evenly: "We know. Right after you left Alvarez and his two aides came here looking for Rodolfo's brother. Luckily, we spotted him just as he was tying up his horse and hid Rodolfo in the back room. Alvarez told us what had happened, and I told him that Rino had not been seen here in weeks, so he darted off."

Carlos got off the cart and motioned towards the trough, ready to water Raquel. Sister Simona warned: "Raquel and you better get some rest. First light tomorrow you'll need to make an emergency trip to Yara!"

Chapter 14

Pilón - Yara, August, 1859: A Quick Return

As long as you are in my life, I will continue to love you with the hope that you will someday return the unconditional love I feel for you.
Alyssa Perkins

"**B**ut I've got to help my brother!" protested Rodolfo.

"If you stay around here, they'll most likely get you before you find Rino!" countered Sister Simona sternly. "Go back to the farm, we'll send word if we learn anything. Rino has broken the law and sooner or later he'll feel the garrote around his neck." The nun put her arm over the boy's heaving shoulder and added softly: "Go to the back room and try to catch a few winks. You need to be out of here before anyone spots you. If they do, at a minimum you will end up in an institution."

"I haven't done anything!" continued the young man.

"Leonardo Serrano is a very powerful man. Whether he lives or dies, you and your brother are going to become targets of the revenge of his supporters. You need to be as far from here as possible, right away."

"But I don't want to go…" repeated Rodolfo.

"You have even less of a choice than when we sent you away last month. Get away or get killed or sent to an orphanage."

Rodolfo tried to continue resisting, but he was too weary. He turned around and retreated to the sick room.

Just before dawn, Sister Simona went to wake him up. He was dressed and sitting on the cot, holding a crumpled piece of paper. "You need to do this for me, again!" he begged.

"Another letter for Carmela Serrano?" questioned the nun, incredulously.

"Yes. Promise that you will have it delivered to Carmela's slave, or I'll have to do it myself."

Sister Simona again knew she had no choice. If Rodolfo set foot in the market, it would be his end.

Silently, she picked up the paper and read:

> "*Dear Carmela,*
>
> > *I have no words to tell you how sorry I am for the terrible deed my brother has committed against your mother and uncle. Please believe me, I had nothing to do with it, it was a senseless act of revenge on Rino's part. I must go away again, without even having been able to see you. As I said earlier, I do not know when, but I will be back. I love you, and some day, God permitting, I will make you my wife. Please think of me without anger.*
>
> > *Until next we see each other. I love you more than words can express.*
>
> > *Yours,*
> > *Rodolfo*"

***

Manolo and Isabel were taken aback by Rodolfo's sudden return to *Los Suspiros*, but tried to offer some consolation to the youth, whose face was a desolate mask of exhaustion, concern, and regret. "I meant what I said about your being welcome back here" insisted Manolo. "But we are all going to have to work extra hard. We are shorthanded and I need to buy a new mule … and another shotgun."

Chapter 15

Pilón, August, 1859: A Divided Family

All happy families resemble one another, but each unhappy family is unhappy in its own way.
Leo Tolstoy

The Serranos presented a common front to the world in the aftermath of the attack that wounded Cecilia and left Leonardo on the verge of death. The mother, physically hurting and morally outraged, condemned Rino's attack as an unforgivable non-Christian act. "They should shoot that bastard on sight and spare the town the trouble of a trial," she would repeat to anyone within earshot. The children outwardly concurred with her mother, adding to their grievances against Rino a concern for her recovery from the shoulder wound.

Indoors, however, their unanimity fractured. Graciela had little interest in family affairs, but was loyal to her mother and was genuinely outraged that someone would dare to shoot at them. Alberto felt guilty about indirectly unleashing the chain of events that had led to the attack on Rino and his revenge, but sympathized with his former friend's rage, though could not condone the attack on his uncle. Carmela was the sole dissenter: her uncle had brought the shooting on himself by the cowardly assault that left Rino scarred for life. "Leonardo is a prick and deserved what he got" she would start, and usually end, sharp arguments with her mother.

The dispute festered with the passage of time, for the authorities were unable track down the criminal despite sending search parties through a good part of the Sierra Maestra's western mountains. Meanwhile, Leonardo's condition showed no improvement: the bullet had lodged near the spine, and it was not feasible to operate to remove it. He remained an invalid, suffering from a great deal of pain and unable to continue to run the mill's affairs.

Cecilia would have moved back to La Habana and left Pilón and its sorrows behind, but Leonardo could not be moved without great risk to his life, and the mill–which now was being offered for sale–had to continue to operate, managed by her with the assistance of Leonardo's secretary, who was the mill's administrator. It was an uneasy paralysis, which aggravated the conflict among the family members.

One evening as they shared another unenjoyable meal, Graciela made an announcement: "Living in this house is not pleasant anymore. I'm going to move in with my friend Ernestina Cueto. They have a spare room in their home, and I will enjoy the company of the Cuetos better than the funeral atmosphere here."

"You didn't ask whether I approved of such move, which I don't think is appropriate under the circumstances."

"Mother, I am eighteen years old. I need no permission to move anywhere I damned please."

"Don't you dare challenge your own mother!" warned Cecilia, raising her voice.

"I will, if that's what it takes to become independent."

"Graciela, decent girls only leave their homes to get married. What you are talking about doing would be a scandal. You would add shame to all the grief our family is going through right now," the mother wailed.

"How and where I live is nobody's business. I'm not going to let the gossips in your sewing circle rule my life."

"Well, if you choose to leave, don't count on getting any support from me!"

"I don't need your money. I still have the trust that father set up for me when he died a decade ago. When that runs out, or even before, I will get a job to support myself."

"A job? Like the peons? A girl of a good family working? Out on the streets like a puta?"

"I'm no whore. I can get a job as a teacher any day I want. God knows the schools in this dump of a town could use somebody qualified to teach letters to the local boys and girls."

"Well, do as you want. I have no time to deal with your caprice."

"Don't worry, I will."

Chapter 16

Pilón, September, 1859: Finding a New Friend

Each new friendship can make you a new person because it opens up new doors inside of you.
Kate DiCamillo

Alberto spent some time searching through Pilón's young male population for more reliable friends than the disappeared Durán brothers. His efforts proved, for the most part, unsuccessful. Most of the town's teenage population consisted of barely educated or illiterate members of the lower classes, already earmarked for a brutish life as farm hands or laborers at the mill.

There was one notable exception, however: Carlos Rafael ("Carlitos") Masó, a descendant of a family of means that owned a large farm in

85

Yara. Carlos and his mother had moved to Pilón when she separated from her husband Rafael on account of his frequent infidelities and lived off an inheritance she had received from her father. Mother and son were reasonably well-to-do; Carlitos was an alert and pleasant young man who was well above Alberto's usual football-playing buddies.

Alberto and Carlitos met by accident during one of Alberto's excursions to the mountains that rose behind the town. Alberto was following his favorite trail, climbing sharply towards the mountain peaks, when, taking a sharp turn of the road, he nearly collided with another boy who stood in the middle of the path watching intently to the woods above through a pair of binoculars.

"Pardon me" apologized Alberto. "I did not expect running into anyone way out here."

"No problem" replied Carlitos. "I came here whenever I to watch the birds."

"What birds?" asked Alberto, who was largely ignorant of the wildlife of the Sierra Maestra.

"All kinds of birds!" replied Carlitos enthusiastically. "There are always dozens of birds flying around this area. See?" He handed to binoculars over to Alberto and pointed to a tall pine that rose across the trail. On the irregular crown of the tree was perched a spectacular bird with blue and white feathers and a deep red chest that sat placidly but, from time to time, uttered a pleasant "toco-toco-tocoro-tocoro..." call.

"Coño, que lindo" declared Alberto. "What's it called?"

"They call it a tocororo because of the way it sings," replied Carlitos. "And that's not the only nice bird you can see…"

***

That chance encounter evolved into a solid friendship. The two boys, who were of similar age (Carlitos was just one year older than Alberto), had similar interests in literature, sports, and music, and both were starting to think about girls and wonder about their future. As they became more trusting of one another, they discovered they had another, potentially more dangerous interest in common. Since he had witnessed as a young boy Narciso López's execution Alberto had been dissatisfied with the oppressive Spanish rule of its last major colony in the Americas; Carlitos had confided that he harbored similar feelings.

"Why don't you come with me to Manzanillo sometime?" asked Carlitos one afternoon. "Mom sends me there every once in a while, to spend time with my father and my two uncles, Bartolomé and Isaías."

"What's in Manzanillo for me?" queried Alberto.

"It is a nice town. And it has a new logia."

"What's a logia?"

"It's like a social club. I can't tell you more, because I don't exactly know. I'm not old enough to join, but my father and uncles are members and speak highly of their logia, although they don't discuss the details of what they do."

"But if you are too young to belong, so would I" objected Alberto.

"But you can still come visit my folks and hear some interesting things."

"Well, it seems rather mysterious, but I would go, just to keep you company. When are you going?"

"Next couple of weeks. I'll let you know."

***

The *Tropical Star No. 4* Masonic Lodge was too small and recently established to have a permanent site. Its couple of dozen members were all male, educated, reasonably well-to-do residents of the coastal area of the Santiago de Cuba province that ran from the mouth of the Cauto River to Cabo Cruz. Most resided in or around Manzanillo. For that reason, the Lodge's meetings took place in a private room in Manzanillo's largest tavern.

Neither Carlitos (age 15) nor Alberto (14) would be allowed to attend November's meeting of the Manzanillo Lodge. However, they stayed at the tavern as guests of Rafael Masó, Carlitos' father, and sat through the backroom discussion the three brothers held–assisted by large amounts of Rioja–concerning the political issues that were brought up during the meeting. Bartolomé, as usual, led the discussion:

"I must be the only one around here that is pessimistic about the change in governor. It is perhaps good that Prime Minister O'Donnell decided to replace butcher Concha with his protégé Francisco Serrano (not related to Alberto's family), but I doubt that the new governor will be any better for Cuba than his predecessor. All that Madrid cares for is bleeding us dry and whoever is in charge here will only implement the dictates of the Court."

Alberto did not follow the details of the discussion that ensued, but he remembered well that Concha had been governor when Narciso

López had attempted to invade Cuba. Concha had quashed the invasion and put López and the other conspirators to death by garrote, a gruesome event that had been engraved in Alberto's memory. Serrano, whoever he was, had to be an improvement over Concha.

Something about the conversation, however, stayed with Alberto: the people who belonged to this Lodge were passionate about how their land was ruled and what the future held for them and the rest of the inhabitants of Cuba. He had never contemplated becoming involved in politics as a part of his life, but now realized that in the future, it would be as important, perhaps, as playing ball or gazing at pretty girls.

Chapter 17

Pilón, December, 1859: Holiday Cheer

Christmas is not a time or a season but a state of mind.
Calvin Coolidge

Christmas that year was a joyful holiday for many people in Pilón. With the growth in the sugar industry, economic conditions were good despite the poor administration of the colonial government. Salaries and the Christmas holiday bonus allowed the sugar mill workers to have a plentiful feast for their special Nochebuena dinner: the smell of roasting pork permeated throughout town.

The Serrano family was holding a holiday reception on Christmas Eve. Cecilia was not in the mood for celebrations but felt obliged to invite the families of the key mill employees in addition to public officials (all Spaniards, as government jobs at all levels tended to be). Wine and hard liquors flowed freely and hired servers made the rounds offering pastelitos de carne (meat pastries), crab croquettes, deviled ham sandwiches, and other delicacies, while a hired string quartet played the latest light music straight from Vienna. Cecilia circulated around the salon chatting with the guests while her daughters, enlisted for the occasion, spent time talking with the younger members of the visitors. Christmas Eve was supposed to be a day of fasting, but everyone in Cuba skirted the ecclesiastical command by feasting and serving dinner late that evening, after which many of the faithful (mostly the ladies) would take a leisurely walk to help digest their dinner. They would proceed to the church where they would sit through the Misa del Gallo, the midnight mass ushering Christmas day.

Carmela was chatting with some girls from their social circle when Yaya approached her and whispered, "Pardon me, my lady, but there is someone at the door asking for you." She was visibly upset.

"What's the matter?" asked Carmela, puzzled.

Yaya did not respond but walked quickly to the

front door and opened it slightly. Rodolfo Durán, pale as a ghost, took a step forward but did not seek to enter the house.

"Rodolfo!" exclaimed Carmela, "What in heaven are you doing here?"

"I've come to get you" he declared in a voice that broke.

"What do you mean?"

"I figured that tonight, of all nights, everyone else would be busy with other things and it would be safe for me to come see you."

Carmela stepped out onto the front porch and confronted the boy. "What do you want? Don't you know the alguaciles have been looking for you and your criminal brother for months?"

"I don't know where Rino is" replied Rodolfo remorsefully. "But I live north of here, and don't plan to ever come back."

"Well, good, because you would not be welcome after what your brother did."

Rodolfo extended his arm and grasped Carmela's elbow. "Would you please walk with me for a few moments?"

Carmela demurred. "I'm busy tonight. We are entertaining half the town."

"I know, but this is important and can't wait. My life depends on it."

Carmela, used to Rodolfo's suicidal pronouncements, stepped onto the porch and then out into the street. "Alright. But we must be quick."

"I want you to marry me" blurted Rodolfo, without preamble.

"What? Have you lost your mind?"

"No. Listen. I have been working on a coffee plantation north of here. The owner died suddenly a few days ago and his widow, whose son has moved permanently to Europe, does not want to sell the farm and has offered me to become her partner and assume responsibility for the plantation's operations. It is a lot of work, but I will be making good money for the foreseeable future." He paused to catch his breath.

"What does that have to do with me?" asked Carmela coldly.

"Now I can afford to provide you with a comfortable life, just like you deserve."

There was a pause while Carmela tried to digest the new information. "So, you are saying that you feel you can now support me properly. Therefore, I should marry you?"

"Exactly!"

"What makes you think I would want to marry you, even if you offered me a castle in Spain?"

"Because I love you, I know you at least like

me, and I know you are not happy living with your shitty family!"

"Curb your tongue! I love my family!"

"You yourself have told me that you despise your uncle and don't get along with your mother or your sister. What's holding you here?"

"I have had differences with everyone but Albertico, but that doesn't mean I'm ready to bolt away."

"With me you would be able to do as you pleased and wouldn't have to feel guilty about the terrible things your uncle does. You would be able to start a new life, be your own person, be free! You'll never be able to do this as long as you live under that roof, and you will end up marrying a pot-bellied Gallego smelling of garlic who will treat you as a slave."

"You give me no credit for being able to fight for myself."

"And do what? You are a prisoner here in Pilón and will never escape."

"Come on" replied Carmela with irritation. "You exaggerate."

"You know in your heart I'm right."

There was another pause. They stood under a tallow lamp streetlight that cast a feeble, flickering illumination to the night. Despite the uncertain light, Rodolfo could notice how the expression on Carmela's face shifted from defiance to regret. Finally, she broke the silence. "Anyhow, the most important problem is that I don't love you. At best, you have been a friend. Nothing more."

Rodolfo could barely hide his smile. "But you do! How many times have we sat on that bench in the church's garden? How many times have you poured your soul into mine, and I trusted you with my all my wishes and fears?" He took her hand, and she did not pull back.

He caressed her hand and lowered his voice so it became a whisper. "You know I love you like nobody has before and never will. Trust your heart and come with me."

Carmela started to pull away to free herself, when an angry voice sounded behind them, by the front door: "Carmela, where are you and what are you doing?" It was Cecilia, summoning her daughter to return to give service at the party.

Carmela responded in the impulsive way of all her dealings with Rodolfo. "I've had it here! Let's go!"

Rodolfo led her into the night to the next corner where a lit lamp sat on the ledge of a building wall. He retrieved the lamp with one hand and led Carmela with the other.

"Where are we going?"

"To the church, where else? Father Pastor is waiting."

***

Father Pastor stood in the nave of the church in the company of his altar boys and a man that Carmela at first did not recognize. "Finally," the man remonstrated, and Carmela recognized him: it was Carlos, the black slave who worked for the nuns that ran the emergency care unit. "Does your mistress know you are here?"

"I left for Manzanillo two days ago. As far as Sister Simona knows, I'm still there. When I return, I'll tell her that the cart lost a wheel, and it took me a long time to get it repaired."

"Will she believe you?"

"I hope she does. If not, I will be sold to some sugar cane farmer."

"Well, Father, it took some doing" said Rodolfo sheepishly. "But we are here now!"

Father Pastor cleared his throat. "I didn't think this was going to happen. Let's not waste any more time. Sooner or later, someone is going to come looking for this girl. I want you out of here before they arrive."

The ceremony was brief. When it was over, the priest declared:

"I will probably be run out of town for this, but you are now man and wife. Love each other and be faithful. May the Lord bless your union." He made the sign of the cross and waved them away.

Carlos led the way to the back of the church building, where a mule and cart waited for them. "It's going to be a difficult drive, going out on the county road in the dark of night. I suggest we stop in Niquero until dawn and then proceed to Manzanillo in the morning."

"I have nothing, nothing!" complained Carmela bitterly as she mounted the cart.

"Don't worry, my dear. You are dressed nicely. We'll buy everything you need in Manzanillo," replied Rodolfo.

It was Carlos this time who repeated Yaya's refrain: "It's madness." And then he added: "But love often is."

Chapter 18

Pilón, December, 1859: Holiday Blues

Christmas is a holiday that persecutes the lonely, the frayed,
and the rejected.
Jimmy Cannon

Cecilia had ample reasons to feel down as the last week of the year came along. Carmela's elopement had filled her with anger and shame, and Graciela's final preparations to leave home were no less depressing for having been announced. Her brother-in-law remained bedridden and in critical condition, leaving her saddled with the task of running a large business, something for which she had no aptitude or interest. Only Albertico remained loyal and affectionate, but apart from his love he was too young to be useful to her at the moment.

She had contacted lawyers in La Habana, tasking them with securing a buyer for *Santa Cruz*. The sugar industry was still expanding wildly in Cuba, and the lawyers had assured her that she would be able to sell the mill and realize a good profit, but warned that finding a buyer or a group of investors with the means and interest in acquiring a property in the eastern end of Cuba might take some time.

Thus, Cecilia found herself almost alone in the drawing room of the manor house on New Year's Eve, waiting to say goodbye to that tumultuous year and hoping for better times to come.

Albertico sat next to her on the blue velvet divan. They were eating canapes and drinking champagne (for which the boy, not yet of age, had received a special dispensation). Before them, in a low table, sat a large bowl full of imported grapes. As the grandfather clock across the room from them ticked away the seconds that remained of the year 1859, Cecilia could no longer hold back her tears.

"How I missed your father, darling. If Lázaro had been alive, none of this would have happened! This family is in such a mess…!" She clutched her son to her breast. "Promise you will stay with me…